This igloo book belongs to:

....

Contents

igloobooks

Published in 2015
by Igloo Books Ltd, Cottage Farm, Sywell, NN6 0BJ
www.igloobooks.com

Illustrated by Ela Jarzabek. Additional colour by Natalie and Tamsin Hinrichsen
Written by Melanie Joyce

Cover designed by Vici Watson
Interiors designed by Kerri-Ann Hulme
Edited by Stephanie Moss

LEO002 1115
2 4 6 8 10 9 7 5 3 1
ISBN 978-1-78557-047-6

Printed and manufactured in China

Stories for 4 Year Olds

igloobooks

Birthday Surprise

On Mummy's birthday, Tilly wanted to make something **great**.

Then **suddenly**, Tilly had an idea of what she could create.

She put on her T-shirt and her rainbow shorts.

Then, Tilly went to the cupboard and pulled out all sorts.

There were pens and paints and paper galore.
Tilly spread them all over the floor.

SPLAT!
went the pink paint,
the red and the blue.

SPLODGE!
went the tissue paper,
glitter and glue.

"Mummy!" called Tilly.
"I've got something for you."

Mum **gasped** when she saw the state of Tilly.
She started to laugh and Tilly felt **silly**.

"I made this for you,
Mummy," she said.
"For your birthday...

... If you don't like it, I'll put it away."

"It's **fantastic!**" said Mum. "I love every single part.
The best bit is you, Tilly. You're a work of art!"

Tilly had glitter on her hands
and all over her nose.

She had paint in her hair
and all down her clothes.

"Thank you, Tilly," said Mum. "It's the most **wonderful** card. You're very kind and you've worked so hard.

Now it's upstairs with you and into the tub, to wash all that paint off, **rub-a-dub-dub**."

8

Mum was happy and Tilly was happy, too.
She'd had fun with her paints, her brushes and glue.
Mum thought Tilly was terribly clever.
She was definitely having the **best** birthday ever!

Dan's Dinosaur

DING-DONG! went the doorbell on Dan's birthday.

It was a parcel from his grandad. He lived **very** far away.

Dan **tore** off the wrapping paper, his eyes open wide.
Dan gasped at the **magic** dinosaur book inside.

"**Cool!**" said Dan. He quickly **dashed** off with the book.
He ran up to his bedroom, to take a good look.

In the book, some dinosaurs were **big** and others were small.
"They're brilliant," thought Dan.
"I like the baby ones best of all."

"I wish, I wish," he said,
"that I had my own dinosaur."
Suddenly...

... WHOOSH!

The book fell to the floor.

The magic book **gurgled**. It **shivered** and **shook**.
You'll just never guess what came out of that book.

First there was a **leg** and some **feet**. Then pink **toes**.
Then other **legs**, some **spikes**, a **tail** and a **nose**.

13

The thing looked at Dan and it gave a **huge**...

...ROAR!

"**Uh-oh,**" said Dan. "It's a **dinosaur!**"
Downstairs, Mum said, "**What was that?!**"
"**Nothing,**" replied Dan. "I stood on the cat!"

The dinosaur immediately dived into Dan's closet.
Then, it ran out again and left a **smelly** deposit.
"Ew, **yuck!**" cried Dan, holding his nose.

"I'll have to be **very** careful where that dinosaur goes."

The dinosaur **thundered** down the stairs to the hall.
It **shook** all the furniture and the pictures on the wall.
It ate all the cat's biscuits and even Dan's sister's toys.

"Oh, Dan," said Dad.

"Don't make so much **noise!**"

In the kitchen, the dinosaur
ate everything in sight.

He ate all day long... but was
still hungry that night.

So he **chomped** on the quilts... and the carpets, too.

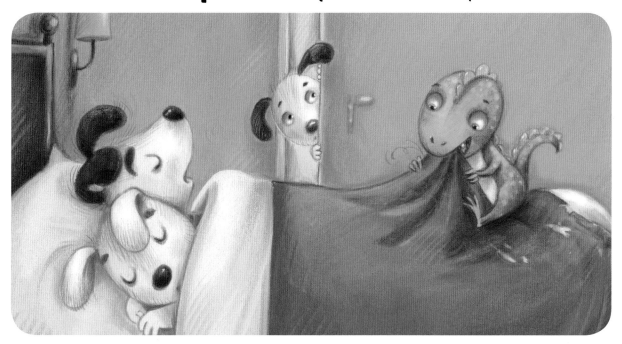

"Oh dear," said Dan. "What am I going to do?!"

Dan took the dinosaur to Dad's garden shed.
"**Settle down**," he said. "**It's time for bed.**"

But that dinosaur **snored**. What a terrible sound.
Everything shook for miles around.

Then, when Dan heard Dad's **angry** voice,
he knew he didn't have a choice.
If Dad opened the shed door to discover...

... a **dinosaur** there, he'd **never** recover.

So, Dan wished the dinosaur back into the book.

FIZZ!

POP!

SWISH!

He didn't dare look.

Just then, the shed door **creaked** open wide.

Dad very carefully stepped inside.

20

"You are up to something, I know," Dad said.
"I think it's time you went back to bed."

Dan smiled secretly and shuffled across the floor.
Never again would he wish for a dinosaur!

If I Were...

If I were a pirate, I'd be **fiercer** than the rest.

I'd fight **scary** sea monsters and find treasure in a chest.

I'd have pirate adventures, but always be home for tea.

"*Arrr!..*"

... I'd say to Mum and Dad. "Here's a present from me!"

If I were a fairy, I would have lovely, **fluttery** wings.
I'd **flit** by pretty flowers and **dance** in enchanted rings.

The other fairies would say, "**Hello**," and give me a special name.
I would be called **Bluebell** and join in their fairy game.

If I were a princess, I'd have a kingdom made of **sweets**. I'd ride on my royal pony giving everybody treats.

I'd wear a diamond tiara and a **sparkly** dress. "Your Highness," my subjects would say.

"You're a **beautiful** princess."

If I were an explorer, I'd go where no one had gone before.

Then, I'd find a dinosaur that...

...growled and snarled and...

... roared!

I'd take him home to play with, so I would never be bored.

If I were a ballerina, I would wear my **best** tutu.
I'd show my ballet teacher all the steps that I could do.

"You're amazing," she would say. "The leading part is yours."
Then I'd dance in the ballet show to everyone's applause.

If I were a magician I'd do some amazing magic tricks. My friends would come to me for things they wished to fix.

I'd turn Molly into a fairy...

... and give Josh a new football.

Then I'd **magic** up a feast...

... and a playground for us all.

The Golden Rocket

Roger was digging in the garden when he found a rocket.
He rummaged for his handkerchief and pulled it from his pocket.

He rubbed and scrubbed it until it **shone** and **gleamed**.

"**Cripes!**" said Roger.
"It's gold!"

But the rocket wasn't what it seemed.

That night, in bed, when Roger should have been tucked up tight, a noise by the wardrobe woke him up. **CLICK!** He switched on the light.

The rocket **buzzed** and **whirred**.

It **trembled**, **wobbled** and **shook**.

Curious, Roger climbed out of bed to take a closer look.

Roger touched the rocket. It went
SPARK, FIZZ, SPUTT and **SWOOSH!**
Suddenly, Roger was inside and it shot off with a **WHOOSH!**

"Hello," said a little voice,
"I'm Arnold. Welcome on-board.
Thank you for rescuing my rocket.
A space trip is your reward."

They flew to the moon and Arnold said,

"Put on this spacesuit, please."

Roger floated about and found the moon really was made of cheese!

VROOM! went the rocket past Venus, **blasting** through the stars.

Roger waved to aliens going on their holidays to Mars.

Roger saw wonderful creatures floating around in space.

On Saturn little aliens were **whizzing** all over the place.

The rocket sped to Arnold's planet, where Roger played with his friends.

"This is such fun!" he said to Arnold. **"I don't want it to end."**

Roger met Arnold's mum and dad. They waved and said, "Hi."
"Stay for tea," said Arnold's dad. "Mum's made meteor pie."

What was in that pie, luckily,
Roger would never know.
Before he took a single bite...

... Arnold said,
"It's time to go."

"Goodbye," said Roger, waving, as the rocket **blasted** away.
"I think space is just **fantastic**. I've had a lovely day."
Arnold flew Roger home, landing on his bedroom shelf.

With a
SPARK...

...FIZZ,

SPUTT...

... suddenly, Roger was his normal self.

He leaned down to the rocket and inside saw a smiling face.

"Thank you, Arnold," he said, as the rocket **roared** back into space.

After that, when Roger saw a **flash** of gold up in the sky, he was sure it was his little friend in his rocket, **flying** by.

My Wishes

If I had **magic** wishes, I know what I would do.
I'd put on my red sneakers and come and call for you.
We'd climb on-board a **shiny** train and take a **magic** ride.
We'd have such **fun** together, sitting side by side.

Choo-choo! we'd chug up to
the **highest** mountaintop.
Slowly over the hill we'd go.
Click-clack, no time to stop.

Whoo-whoo! our train would
whizz and **zoom**, down the other side.
Soon we'd **giggle** and **squeal**
on our roller coaster ride.

I'd wish that I were a **queen** and that you were a **king**.
We'd sit on our royal thrones and **never** do a thing.

Butlers would bring us candy and cakes on silver dishes.
They'd bow and say, **"Yes, Majesties,"** and grant all of our wishes.

We'd ride through an **enchanted** kingdom in a golden coach.
Everyone would **wave** and **cheer** on our approach.

We'd hold a royal garden party and invite them all to tea.
Everyone would have such fun, thanks to **you** and **me**.

I'd wish to have a sleepover, where we **crept** out at night,
with a **magic** lantern, by the full moonlight.

There, we'd meet the fairies. They'd invite us to Fairyland.
We'd have a fairy feast and play in the fairy band.

Then we'd creep back in and **snuggle** up to sleep,
remembering adventures, in our dreams so deep.
I'd **wish** that we could always be together and play.
That you'd be my **special** friend, who **never** goes away.

My Friend Ollie

This is my friend, Ollie, who **no one** else can see.
He doesn't look like **you** and he doesn't look like **me**.
Ollie lives in my wardrobe. He **only** comes out at night.
He **giggles** and **tickles** me and then turns on the light.

I put on my slippers and we carefully **creep**
past the bedroom where Mum and Dad sleep.

Mum **gurgles**.

Dad goes **snort**

and **snore**.

Ollie and me try not to **giggle** as we **scurry** past their door.

CREAK...

... goes each step
on the stair as
we reach the hall.

We **creep** along the carpet...

... towards the kitchen, by the wall.

"**Open**," says Ollie, pointing
at our big fridge door.

We nibble on yummy cupcakes,
but then we just want more.

There's **giggling** and **crunching** and **slurping**.
There's **munching** and **slobbering** and **burping**.
Then, suddenly, there's a voice. It gives me such a fright.

Uh-oh. It's my dad.

CLICK!

On goes
the light.

I try to explain, but it is just as I feared.
When I say, **"Dad it was Ollie!"** he has disappeared.

"Never mind," says Mum. **"Let's just all go to sleep.**
Now upstairs with you and not another peep."

I trudge back up to bed all on my own.
"You've gone and done it again, Ollie!" I groan.
Then I can't help but start to smile.
I know Ollie will be back in just a little while.

47

In bed, I see a shadow move along the floor
and the gentle **thunk** of my wardrobe door.

"Goodnight,
Ollie," I say.

"See you soon."

Then I fall **fast asleep**
by the light of the moon.